At my grandma's house in the village,
I opened my eyes one morning and saw a big. . .

Rangoli

Discovering the Art of Indian Decoration

Anuradha Ananth

ILLUSTRATED BY Shailja Jain

For Kannamama and Devaji Rao Thatha,
Susheela and Saroja Avva — my grandparents,
who mean the world to me — A.A.

Text copyright © Anuradha Ananth 2007
Illustrations copyright © Shailja Jain 2007
The right of Anuradha Ananth to be identified as the author
and of Shailja Jain to be identified as the illustrator of this work
has been asserted by them in accordance with
the Copyright, Designs and Patents Act, 1988 (United Kingdom).

First published in India in 2007 by Tulika Publishers

This edition first published in Great Britain and in the USA in 2011 by
Frances Lincoln Children's Books, 4 Torriano Mews,
Torriano Avenue, London NW5 2RZ
www.franceslincoln.com

A catalogue record for this book is available from the British Library.

ISBN 978-1-84780-179-1

Printed in Dongguan, Guangdong, China by Toppan Leefung Printing Ltd. in February 2011

9 8 7 6 5 4 3 2 1

rangoli!

It was made of rice flour and sugar.

"Food for the ants," said my grandma.

"You do a good deed first thing in the morning,

and make your home look beautiful
at the same time," she said.

Soon I saw rangolis everywhere in the village.

On newly-swept floors.

On the red tiles of courtyards.

On the walls of mud homes.

Around lamps in doorways.

In front of temples.

Even on flower-seller Gangamma's sari.

Where will I do a
rangoli at our flat
in the city?

"Don't worry,"
said Grandma.

"I'll teach you a simple, small rangoli. . .

. . . to fit just outside your door!"